For my alma mater, the University of Florida, and our great sports teams

Library of Congress Cataloging-in-Publication Data:

Arnold, Tedd.
Hooray for Fly Guy! / Tedd Arnold.
   p. cm. -- (Fly Guy ; #6)
"Cartwheel books."
Summary: Fly Guy joins Buzz's football team, despite Coach's
misgivings, and hits the field for a special, secret play.
ISBN 978-0-545-00724-5
[1. Flies--Fiction. 2. Football--Fiction.] I. Title.

PZ7.A7379Hoo 2008
[E]--dc22

                              2007037521

ISBN 978-0-545-00724-5

21 20 19 18   15 16 17 18 19 20 21

Printed in China 38
First printing, September 2008

A boy had a pet fly.
He named him Fly Guy.
Fly Guy could say
the boy's name—

BUZZ!

Chapter 1

Fly Guy went with Buzz
to play football.

Coach said, "We need
one more player for
the big game."

Buzz said,

"Fly Guy can play."

Coach laughed.
"Flies can't play football."

Buzz said, "Fly Guy, show him what you can do."
Fly Guy kicked the ball.

Fly Guy went out for a pass.

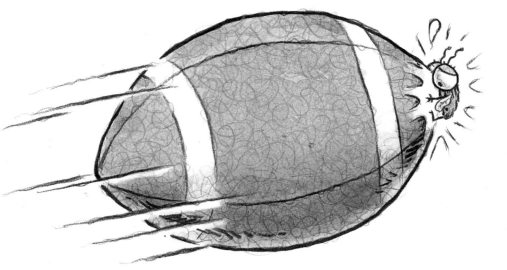

Fly Guy tried to tackle Buzz.

"I was right," said Coach.
"Flies can't play football.
But he can come to the
game."

Chapter 2

It was the day before the big game. Buzz made a helmet for Fly Guy.

They played football.

They did jumping jacks.

They planned a secret play.

They made up a
touchdown dance.

They went to the big game.
Coach said, "A new player
joined our team."

Fly Guy sat on the bench.

The game started.
His team scored.
Fly Guy cheered.

The other team scored.

Fly Guy worried.

The other team scored a lot!

Chapter 3

Finally, there was one second left in the game.

The other team was ahead.
They were about to
score again.

And the new
player was hurt.

Coach said, "Okay, Fly Guy.
You can play now.
The game is lost anyway."

Buzz said, "It's time for our secret play."

Fly Guy went to the line.

The other team snapped
the ball to their quarterback.

Fly Guy flew
fast and straight.

He flew right up the
quarterback's nose!

The boy dropped the ball.

Buzz picked it up and ran.

He scored!

Fly Guy and Buzz did their
touchdown dance.

The team cheered. "We won! Hooray for Fly Guy!"